Children of the Wind and Water

Five stories about Native American children
written by Stephen Krensky
illustrated by James Watling

SCHOLASTIC INC.

New York   Toronto   London   Auckland   Sydney

For Ashley
—S.K.

For Geoffrey in the Kispiox
—J.W.

ISBN 0-590-46963-0

Text copyright © 1994 by Stephen Krensky.
Illustrations copyright © 1994 by James Watling.
All rights reserved. Published by Scholastic Inc.

12 11 10 9 8 7 6 5 4 3 2 1   4 5 6 7 8 9/9

Printed in the U.S.A.   09

First Scholastic printing, November 1994

Introduction

For thousands of years, the only people who lived in North America were Native Americans, a group of people comprised of many different tribes.

Each tribe developed particular skills as influenced by their environment — the rivers, the trees, the land, the sea. Over time, the scattered tribes developed different customs and traditions. Some things, though, they shared in common, especially regarding children. Childhood in every tribe was a mixture of work and play. Skills such as hunting and carving were not learned in schools, but were important parts of daily life.

The following stories recreate some of the experiences of Native American children who lived almost two hundred years ago, a time when their peoples still had much of North America to themselves. And while the world has greatly changed in the past few centuries, we can still learn from the Native American way of life.

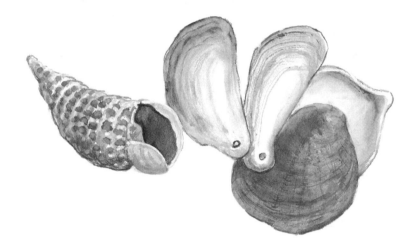

A Muskogee Trader

It was a lazy day on the river. Sweet Water was sitting in the front of the canoe. Her father was paddling in the back. The water was clear and still. There were no stray logs or hungry alligators in sight.

Sweet Water was busy sorting through her shells. She had gathered them at the edge of the great sea. She remembered well the ocean breezes and the crashing waves and the sea gulls swooping overhead. Someday, she hoped, she and her father would return there. They never stayed in one place very long, though. They were river traders, moving from village to village peddling their goods. There were only the two of them now. Her mother had died of a snakebite the year before.

Sweet Water's shells were mostly white. Some were twisted like knotted roots. Others were flat like dried leaves. Often, she strung the best of them together into an armband. It was delicate work. Sweet Water had broken many shells learning how to poke a small hole through the middle.

Up beyond the riverbank, two men were playing a game of *chungke*. A small crowd was watching. The men ran along the grass chasing a flat, rolling stone. Each man then threw a pole at the spot where he thought the stone would stop.

Both the crowd and the players came from an old village just downstream. At a small clearing around the next bend, Sweet Water and her father grounded their canoe. Then they dragged it out of the water. The canoe was their most valuable possession. It had been hollowed out from a fallen cypress tree. Some of the inside had been burned out. The rest had been chipped away with stones.

News of the traders' arrival spread quickly. Several villagers approached with copper and pipestone. They hoped to trade them for something Sweet Water and her father had brought from far away.

Sweet Water's father greeted everyone warmly. It was important to make the villagers feel welcome. Meanwhile, Sweet Water put out salt and dried fish to trade. She also found a good spot to display a shell armband she had finished the day before.

Nobody acted quickly. There was much whispering and

nodding. A trade was not to be hurried. Sweet Water noticed one villager with some fine deerskins slung over his shoulder. They were beautiful, but she knew better than to show any real interest yet.

At first, the villager let others look ahead of him. Finally, he came closer. He picked up a dried fish and sniffed it. Then he dropped it quickly.

Sweet Water covered a smile with her hand. She didn't like dried fish either.

The villager noticed the armband. The white shells were not things he could find in the woods.

Her father had taught Sweet Water to watch faces carefully during a trade. The eyes were especially important. They could tell her when someone was truly ready to trade.

The villager had such a look in his eyes now.

Her father joined them. He explained that Sweet Water had made the armband from rare shells. The shells came from the great sea. To reach it would take a journey of many days.

The villager offered a deerskin in trade.

Sweet Water wanted the deerskin, but she did not accept it. The armband was worth more. The villager could replace the deerskin the next day. She could not replace the shells until her next visit to the great sea.

The villager considered this for a while. Then he offered both deerskins. They were all he had.

Sweet Water looked to her father. The deerskins were soft and a rich brown color. With his approval, the trade was completed.

At last, all the trading was done. Tonight, she and her

father would stay in the village. They would leave tomorrow. Sweet Water's eyes opened wide at the thought. Among the clans of the Muskogee, they could travel for many seasons and never visit the same place twice. In the next village, perhaps she would trade one of the deerskins for some glittery mica or a new kind of bead.

But the other one she would keep for herself.

A Dakota Hunter

Snow was falling steadily as a group of Dakota hunters crossed the plain. Several boys walked among them. The youngest was Dark Cloud.

This was his first buffalo hunt. The harsh wind whipped his deerskin leggings, and the snow stung his cheeks. Dark Cloud ignored them. The wind and cold were not important. He must keep watching and stay alert.

The ground under Dark Cloud's snowshoes was white with powdery snow. Dark Cloud smiled. It was good snow for sledding. His younger sister, Small Foot, would like that.

She had a sled made of four buffalo ribs and a piece of hide. The sled had once been his. He remembered many happy days filled with downhill slides and tumbles.

Up ahead, the hunters stopped. The buffalo herd lay just over the next bluff. The hunters spread out in groups of three and four. They would attack the herd from many points, looking for weakness along the edges.

Dark Cloud knew that a hunter needed to be very careful with buffalo. Many of them were as tall as a man and could weigh as much as ten men together. And a buffalo would defend itself fiercely when attacked. Just last summer, four hunters had been gored on a hunt. Two of them died.

At a hand signal from the chief, the hunters crept toward the herd. Everyone moved slowly, crouching low in their wolfskins. The furs kept everyone warm, but they were also meant to fool the herd. The buffalo might run at the scent of hunters. But they did not fear wolves.

At the base of the bluff, Dark Cloud and three hunters found a buffalo struggling in a snowdrift. It pawed mightily, the breath steaming from its nostrils. But it could not break free.

There was no time to wait. Dark Cloud and the three hunters raised their bows.

Beyond the bluff, two younger buffalo had skittered away from the herd. Two groups of hunters closed in on them. Across the plain, one buffalo charged three hunters, who scattered out of its way.

Soon, several more buffalo lay in the snow. The herd slowly moved on. The hunters backed away and lowered their bows. The hunting for this day was over.

Dark Cloud and the other boys took their places by the fallen animals. The slain buffalo were so large that they had to be cut up and placed on low, wooden frames.

The cutting was done carefully, and nothing was left behind. A buffalo was too valuable to let any of it be wasted. Much of it, of course, was eaten or made into clothing. But the buffalo had other uses as well. Shoulder blades became hoes for farming, and bones were turned into knives or arrow straighteners. Horns were carved into spoons and cups. Teeth decorated necklaces. The Dakota cooked soup in the buffalo's stomach sack and twisted its hair into rope and belts. Even the tail was used — to swat flies.

Several hunters shouted in celebration as they dragged the heavy frames back to camp. Dark Cloud joined in. The hunters had been lucky today. No one had been hurt, and many buffalo had fallen. The story of this hunt would become part of the winter count, the painting that recorded important events in the tribe.

Small Foot, though, would not have to wait for the winter count to learn about the hunt. Dark Cloud would tell her everything as soon as he returned.

Unless she was sledding. Then he would wait until dark.

A Huron Canoe Maker

In a wide clearing by the lake, White Feather added wood to a small fire. She was boiling spruce gum. The gum was bubbling in a birch-bark cooking box. The fire under it had to be tended carefully. If it grew too high, the box would burn. If it fell too low, the spruce gum wouldn't boil at all.

White Feather slowly stirred the spruce gum with a stick. She traced a turtle on its surface. White Feather's family were members of the turtle clan. Other families belonged to the clans of different animals — the wolf, the beaver, the owl, the crane. White Feather liked the turtle best. Turtles were slow, but steady, the way she often felt herself.

Next to the turtle, she drew the canoe her family was now making. She put her brother Red Oak in the back. Whenever they went canoeing together, he always insisted on steering.

They had started building the new canoe a few days earlier. First, her father had driven tall stakes into the ground to mark the canoe's shape. Then he had cut the birch bark for the canoe bottom and sides. Birch bark was used because it could be stripped off the tree in long sheets. It was so thick and tough that water could not leak in.

The cut bark was kept wet so it would not dry out and crack when the wooden frame was placed inside it. The piece for the bottom of the canoe was held down flat with rocks. The side pieces were cut to fit the tapered shape of the canoe.

The sound of chopping drew White Feather's attention. Her father and Red Oak were cutting wood for the canoe's frame with stone axes and wedges. The wood was white cedar, which was light but strong and easy to shape. Once the wood was cut, they would shave the shorter pieces into wooden ribs with a crooked knife. Red Oak was just learning how to handle a knife. He had cut himself once already.

When the spruce gum had boiled, White Feather left it to cool. Then she joined her mother, who was sewing the pieces of bark together.

White Feather began helping her. She took a bone tool to make small holes in the bark. Then she threaded spruce root through the holes. Her mother had taught her to pull the roots until the bark pieces overlapped snugly. It was not good to pull them too tightly, though. Then they would ripple and water could seep through.

When all the pieces were sewn together, White Feather brought over the spruce gum. She and her mother began smearing it over the seams on one side of the canoe. The sticky sap felt strange between White Feather's fingers. Boiling the spruce gum had thickened it, and thicker spruce gum made a better watertight seal.

White Feather worked carefully. She rubbed the gum over every seam and hole so water would have no way to enter.

As the sun set, she and her mother finished. Red Oak and their father stopped as well. In the deepening shadows, it was too easy to make mistakes with a crooked knife.

Tomorrow, White Feather would boil more spruce gum for the other side of the canoe. Her brother and father would shave more wooden ribs. Over several more days, they would fit them into the bark shell. When the canoe was done, the family would use it to hunt and fish and journey over the lake.

White Feather smiled. This time, she hoped to steer the canoe herself.

A Tlingit Carver

Gray Seal sat comfortably under a tree. He was carving a bear mask from a piece of tree stump. He had sharp stone tools, but he was working slowly. The eyes were done and the ears, too. He was having trouble, though, with the nose and mouth. The bear did not look fierce enough.

Gray Seal growled at the mask. Then he felt the lines on his face with his hands. Those were the lines he needed to carve into the mask.

His mother called out to him. It was time to bring some food to his father.

Gray Seal could see his breath before him as he walked up the hill. He felt snug, though, in his deerskin clothes and coat of woven cedar bark. His hands were warm, too, holding the bowl of boiled fish and vegetables.

His father was working on the hilltop. For many days he had been carving a totem pole for Long Shell. She was the richest woman in the village. Gray Seal knew how rich she was by the size of her *labret*. This wooden disk hung from her lower lip. The larger the *labret*, the richer the woman was. Long Shell's *labret* pulled her lip down to her chin.

Gray Seal's father never made totem poles for himself. Other people hired him to make them. Totem poles identified the clan of a house owner, greeted visitors to a village, and even marked the site of an important battle.

At the moment he was carving a raven's head. With steady strokes he shaved slivers from the beak. He used a sharpened bone for the larger work and a small shell for delicate chipping.

The raven was going to be the top of the totem pole. Long Shell belonged to the Raven clan, and all of her family's possessions were marked with a raven. Even her blankets were woven with raven images.

His father stopped to guide Gray Seal's hands over the raven's head. Gray Seal knew he must feel more than the grain of the wood under his fingers. He must feel the shapes within, the shapes a skilled carver could find. A carver did more than just carve, though. He also painted the wood. And he sang and danced to draw the power of the spirits into his work.

After his father finished eating, Gray Seal returned to

their house. It was among several in the village that faced the sea. Gray Seal often collected pieces of wood on the shore. The waves had carved them, he thought, and each piece had a beauty of its own.

Gray Seal had no time now to look for more wood. His father had asked him to make some paints for the totem pole. The painting was always done last, and then the pole would be honored with a *potlatch*. Gray Seal smiled. At a *potlatch* there were always good things to eat, and the host gave presents to everyone.

He ducked under the low opening of his house and went inside. His family shared their house with three other families. Gray Seal gathered some paint ingredients from the platform where he slept. The others he collected from his mother, who was tending the cooking fire.

Many things went into the paint — different kinds of

rock dust, ground-up plants, and animal oils. Gray Seal had learned how to mix them together. He worked carefully. The red paint was not turning out the way he wanted. He added another pinch of salmon eggs. Now a little more fish oil to make it the right thickness.

Finally he stood up and stretched. The paints were ready. They were bright and would last a long time. The totem pole would be pleased to wear them.

Gray Seal was pleased, too. He had made enough paint to decorate the bear's mask as well. It might never actually growl, but it would soon be the fiercest bear in the village.

A Nootka Fisherman

The raindrops were tapping on the wooden roof above Slippery Eel's head. He barely noticed the sound, though. The rain almost never stopped this time of year.

It was dark inside the lodge. Slippery Eel lit an *oolichan*, an oily fish that burned with a soft light. He sat down on a reed mat and began oiling a wooden shaft. It was part of a spear used to hunt whales. The oil helped protect the wood from the salty sea water.

Slippery Eel ran his finger along the shaft. It was almost as tall as two men. He could barely lift it. The end was tipped with a sharpened mussel shell. The shell was tied to the shaft with pine and gum and whale sinew.

His father had told him all about whale hunts. The men approached a whale from many canoes. The chief spear thrower approached first. He stood up in the canoe and plunged his spear into the whale's side. Then each hunter took his turn.

The whale would try to dive or swim away, but it could not escape. The spear heads were made to break off when the whale struggled. They were each attached to long lines tied to inflated sealskins. Dragging them through the water exhausted the whale. Eventually the fight would end.

Slippery Eel heard a shout. He looked outside where his brother and sister were playing with their friends. They were divided into two teams. One team guarded a buried clamshell at the top of a sand pile. The other team tried to capture it.

Slippery Eel did not have time for games now. He finished oiling his father's spear and picked up a smaller one of his own. It was time to go fishing. Sometimes he caught fish with nets and hooks or even a pointed rake. But the spear was his favorite.

He made his way to a narrow wooden bridge over the river. Below it was a pole fence, a wall of sticks stretching from one riverbank to the other. Water and small fish could pass easily through the fence. Larger fish could not, but this didn't keep them from trying.

Slippery Eel spotted a large fish trying to squirm through. He knelt down for a closer look. It was a salmon, a big one as long as his arm.

Slippery Eel raised his spear. He watched closely, moving the spear in time with the fish.

Then he threw it.

The spear missed. The salmon's movements were hard to predict. It wriggled in unexpected ways.

He tried again and missed again. This salmon was like a dancer darting through the water.

One more try. He had it.

The salmon did not give up easily, though. It thrashed about, pulling off the spearhead. But, like the larger whale spears, this spearhead was connected to the shaft by a line. The salmon could not escape.

Still, the fish was strong. Back and forth it swam, pulling Slippery Eel along the bridge. Twice it almost yanked him right into the water.

Finally, the salmon grew tired and Slippery Eel pulled it out of the water. The salmon was the largest fish he had ever caught with a spear.

Someday he would hunt whales, too. Now, though, he would need all his strength just to get the salmon home. He and his family would have a feast tonight.

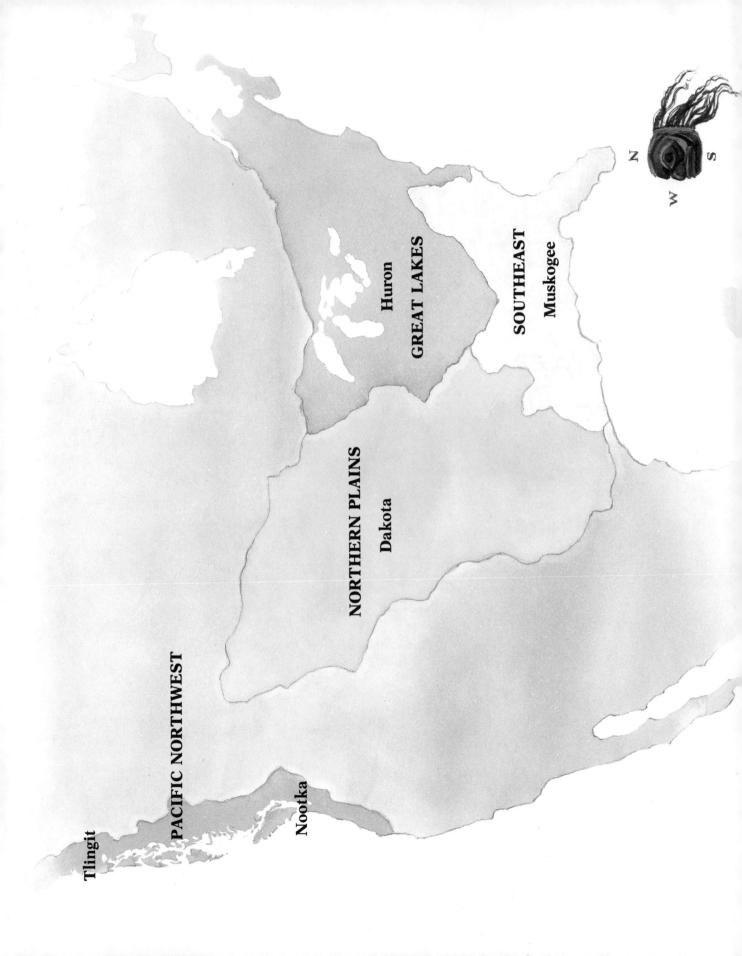

Glossary

The **Muskogees** were a diverse people of the Southeast. Their many villages shared a trading network that stretched east of the Mississippi River to the sea.

Muskogee *chickee*

The **Dakotas** were part of the Sioux family whose tribe roamed the Northern Plains. The Dakotas relied on buffalo for many of their daily needs.

Dakota *tipi*

The **Hurons** of the Great Lakes were skilled woodland dwellers, who often moved with the seasons. They were as comfortable walking a trail on land as they were navigating a river.

Huron *wigwam*

The **Tlingits** lived in the Pacific Northwest, where winters were long and summers were short. They often traveled along the coast sharing customs with both friends and enemies among other Pacific tribes.

Tlingit house

The **Nootkas** of the Pacific Northwest were one of the few seafaring Native American peoples and may have been the only tribe to hunt whales regularly.

Nootka big-house